CHERRY

CANADA

WAY
LIQUOR
MART

Edited by Jon Paul Fiorentino & Andy Brown
Design and cover images by Andy Brown
Interior photos by Dale Stevenson (pages 31, 34, 54, 98, 105)
& Jon Paul Fiorentino (pages 2-3, 43, 62, 120)
Author photo by Karen Paquin

First Edition

This is a work of fiction. Any resemblance to persons living or dead is purely coincidental.

National Library of Canada Cataloguing in Publication

Mayor, Chandra, 1973-
Cherry / Chandra Mayor.

ISBN 1-894994-02-7

I. Title.

PS8576.A958C44 2004 C813'.6 C2004-900812-9

Dépot Legal, Bibliothèque nationale du Québec
Printed in Quebec on recycled paper

CONUNDRUM PRESS
PO Box 55003, CSP Fairmount
Montreal, Quebec, H2T 3E2, Canada
conpress@ican.net http://home.ican.net/~conpress

This book was produced with the financial assistance of the Canada Council for the Arts and the Department of Canadian Heritage through IPOLC.

CHERRY

a novel by

Chandra Mayor

CONTENTS

DEPARTURE

This city settles and shifts on an infrastructure of graffiti, carports, the garish murals sucking on the underbellies of bridges. This city is a stuttering story punctuated by hotel gargoyles and stop signs and the gaping o of the burned out cathedral. It holds you in its grey asphalt arms as you stumble home from the all night café, over the bridges with railings like shattered teeth.

This city settles you in a bed in a room in a brown box and you are indistinguishable from anyone else. This city is full of brick boxes, brown, red, grey, black names with broken letters arching over the doorways. Cockroaches and silverfish skitter beneath the floorboards hoarding crumbs and brackish water, denizens of the dark. The sun loiters for days in the zenith of sky and everyone's arms are brown and spotted, red and peeling.

This city catches your arm in the automated wheeze of a bus door, your foot in the spring pothole. It snags in your hair like the sharp edges of dry leaves. This city's story is written on bus shelters in thick black marker, it is fingered on sidewalks in wet cement, the shallow signatures hidden and cracking in the winter freeze. You are walking on pebbles and bones and the sound of your feet is lost in the rush of cars on the road. A siren wraps itself around your head and the traffic pulls over to the curb, the grey spine of road suddenly bare.

There is always someone watching you in this city, someone who remembers you from five years ago, eight, twelve. You are never allowed to be blank, alone, and everyone is careful not to brush against you on the bus. People are sleeping in the heated bus shelters and you cautiously step around them, your boot longing for the impact. This city stands alone for hours in every direction, escape is never easy, anonymity is never possible, you cannot fall in or out unnoticed.

This flat city is a spring-loaded trap, it closes its teeth around you and you retrace the same routes endlessly, pinned beneath the weight of repetition. The skin under your arms cries salted tears every July and every February the grey sky closes in around your head as you stand in front of the bus depot whispering Calgary, Vancouver, Carolina.

BROADWAY

Broadway is the street where Carly and I live in our first apartment. We take the bus and move her records and stereo from her foster home to the sunsoaked hardwood floors and empty rooms of our new home. We sing Cat Stevens songs on the street amid the blazing trees. I sleep on a futon in the kitchen, and we blacken all the knives, keep a plastic bottle top on the window ledge beside the stove. We don't let our friends come over without food, and we keep our money in a Tupperware container in the linen closet. One night I lie in bed with a man or a boy and listen to the screams of a girl being raped down the hall and I am afraid that it will be my turn next. Carly wants to kick the shit out of the guy but it's the landlord and I am afraid we'll get kicked out so I beg her not to. We burn incense and drop out of school and talk until dawn and eat Froot Loops for dinner. We argue about the dishes and shatter a plate on the red element and it sounds like gunfire. Someone throws a beer bottle at my head and it splinters against the wall and becomes embedded in the plaster, a brown glass mosaic that I can not read.

Lina and Carly and I meet in a park in the summer, then walk downtown and drink coffee until our hands shake in the round diner beneath the parkade on Garry. Lina knows the owner and he won't let us pay. I know that she will make all of this, all of us, into art. Black beetles scurry across the downtown sidewalks and we step around them. We surrender to the secret mapping of walk/don't walk signs blinking in the summer night. The walking person lures us on, the red hand turns us away. We believe in fate and flight. Lina knows the combination of elevators and stairs to get to the roof of the Marlborough hotel and we caress the stone gargoyles in silence, stand and spread our arms like white spines of wings. We wait for the sick lurch deep in our stomachs as we close our eyes and lean down into the night air, thick and blue as paint. Our feet also find the green Provencher bridge, the back fire escape of the Cauldron, and the black ledge of the billboard with cardboard diamonds on the roof of the Dark O'Clock in the Village. We believe in heights and revelations. Fish or cars or pavement or pedestrians: the destination doesn't matter, only the possibility of descent, the thrill of impact, the kiss of sidewalk, river, road, flying up to greet us. Carly says she'll write a song, that her guitar strings will vibrate with our breath. I tell Lina that I'll write us into a poem, that we'll live forever. When Lina moves to Surrey she gives me a painting of a walking figure engulfed in flames. Only the sensation of cool metal beneath my bare feet at midnight takes away the burning, this flat city bleeding light for miles in every direction.

The first time that Carly and I drop acid it is February and luminous snow flashes iridescent in the darkness outside the window of our Broadway apartment. We bought the little white squares from the waiter at the Blue Note. He calls an hour after we drop, repeats back everything we say to him, trying to freak us out but we know it's him and we think it's terribly funny. Everything is terribly funny. We breathe in time to the walls and we decide never to leave our apartment again. We concoct elaborate plans to replenish our acid and cigarette supply, we chain-smoke cigarettes and light incense and discover that we can't eat. The Blue Note waiter stops by our apartment. He sits on our couch and scowls and tells us about his stomach ailments while we laugh and offer him food because, of course, we don't need it anymore. We decide that men are incomprehensible, the way they hit each other to be friendly, and we write it all down because no one has ever thought these things before. We can see the lines of our conversation create a prism across the room despite the shaking, despite the gut rot, and I have never felt so full of love and Carly and I are never going to leave each other ever.

Carly and I pass a bottle of peach schnapps back and forth between us. There is nothing else as sweet as this burn. We are sitting on the concrete steps behind the Blue Note. Carly works there as a busser, clearing the contents of tables into a bin by amber candlelight. James is singing with his guitar on the stage and I have been writing poetry on napkins for hours. Carly's shift ends at 4 AM and we know everyone at every table. The smoke from Carly's cigarette weaves into the worm-eaten leaves of the tree that grows out back. The dish-pig slices his hand open on a broken glass hidden deep in the sink and there is suddenly blood everywhere and Carly is probing the wound, saying, *You gotta see this.* I can see the bone in the centre of his finger and I feel sick. The kitchen has to be cleaned and we won't leave until at least 5, when the sky is striped with salmon. Drunk, we'll stumble to the all-night restaurant up the street with a couple of the waiters. Carly will get sick in the bathroom, and the Blue Note waiters will break the loops on her jeans, dragging her out, yelling, *Don't have the French toast!* The empty bottle of schnapps is in my bag, it jostles and rolls and could shatter at any moment. I'm tired and laughing and stuck in the middle of the story and I can't recognize the brevity of the sweetness of this night.

The kitchen is always blue with smoke, thick enough to taste. It settles in the corners of your eyes, the delicate folds of your ears. It's always trapped in the crevices of skin between your fingers which are always holding knives, blackened tip to blackened tip. You point them away from your body and they are an arrow choosing someone else. The top of your head is always lifting off while your limbs grow heavy, your bones bloated with smoke. Someone's lips are always drawn into an o, their blackened lungs taut and full. There is always someone hungry for the smoke. There is always someone hungry. Knives are always poised in the coils of an element and you are always surrounded by little brown balls. Your fingers are always aching for silver and release.

It is April and for once the snow has melted and spring whispers verdant promises in all the trees, small insects tunnel through the bark, and old men are sleeping on park benches. I am sitting on the grass in Library Park and writing poems in a green spiral notebook. I meet Tom for the first time. He is a friend of Barbara, he is tattooed, he is lean and spare because he is a junkie but I don't know this yet. He says he cares about poetry and he likes my poem and he knows how I feel and I forget that the only reason he knows is because I opened my notebook to him. He says he'll hold me through the night and I believe him. He gives me his phone number and I call him three days later, Earth Day. We go to the Forks and he writes our initials on a tower. They're probably still there. We go back to his place and everyone finds an excuse to come up to his room to view me. I already have a nickname, they call me the princess because I have long brown hair like Rapunzel leaning from her tower window. We are on the third floor and the sun slants in behind the eaves. There are brambles around the house although I can't see them yet. I let Tom crawl into my life as surely as I sit on this green blanket on the bed eating Kraft Dinner and wondering if my life is about to start.

LANGSIDE

Langside is the street where there is a rooming house for punks, where we see demons in the kitchen and write stories on the ceiling in thick black marker. An unknown alphabet in razor red rises on Carly's arm one day when we are high. We copy it down before it bleeds away and we take turns deciphering it. We share stolen menthol cigarettes and a bathroom. Someone steals my shoes and someone regularly ODs. The hospital is around the corner, a short walk on our own feet, a two hour journey with a deadweight friend or acquaintance. No one has a television but we have Op Ivy and a woman who chases her boyfriend down the street with a broken bottle in her hand while he crouches behind cars and apologizes. We laugh because it hurts so much. The landlord pays us to burn the house down for the insurance money and the police drive me to my parents' house at 6 AM.

That first night on Langside Tom and I stay up all night, talking. He tells me about the ghost of the little boy that's supposed to float through the upstairs hallways. We both laugh because the blood pulses so strongly through our muscle and tissue, our bones are so heavy and white, we are too alive for ghost stories. He pulls a dandelion out of thin air behind my ear and I am captivated. We lean into each other at exactly the same moment and our lips meet and I have never been so soft and so hungry. Tom's electric palm presses against the small of my back and it burns as I free-fall. We lie on the bed next to each other and I tell him everything and he doesn't interrupt and I have never been safer than I am now, encircled in his arms. He holds me all night long just like he promised and at some point I fall asleep and at some point I wake up and I am still here, he is still here and the moon drips soft yellow light onto both of us, and I think *yes, now.*

You don't need a jacket for the first time in months, your hands are bare and your arms swing. Spring creeps through this city, small lakes claim the back alleys and brown patches of grass mottle the snow. Every corner of this city is banked with slush and the wind blows abandoned sand into the corners of your eyes. The air in this city caresses your face and the sidewalks are filled with people and dogs. You stand on your porch in socks and the metal mailbox is warm to the touch. Your fingers close around someone else's and everyone in this city has a new lover and the leafless trees whisper *yes, yes, now*.

Tom loves my poems. He thinks they're beautiful. He says, *They're beautiful, you're beautiful.* I come over one night and he has a present, wrapped in old Christmas paper, waiting for me in the middle of the bed. He is smiling. He dances me around the little room. He can't wait for me to open it. I start to peel at the tape and he says, *No no, rip it*, and so I do, like a little kid. There are bits of paper all over the floor and Tom sticks the bow on top of my head. I can feel something smooth and supple beneath the cheap paper and suddenly I am holding it in my hands, it's a leather journal, fat with creamy thick pages. I don't know where he got the money to buy it but I don't care because it's so beautiful. *It's for us,* he says, *I mean it's for you. It's for you to write poems in, poems about us, it's for you to write our story*. I dig a pen out of my purse, I open the front cover and write 'our story' and the date on the first page. Tom is still grinning and the book is heavy in my hands, covered with our fingerprints.

It is morning and I am the only one awake in this house. I pull the hair back from Tom's ear to kiss it softly as he sleeps, my kiss a promise, a benediction. On the soft lobe of his right ear is a small tattoo that I've never seen before, a little blue swastika. He has other tattoos, a spider web on his left elbow, dragons, barbed wire, animals, blue and orange and black. But I've never noticed this before. I sit in the chair across the room, knees pulled up to my chin. When he wakes up I ask him what it means. He looks out the window. He says he was fourteen and stupid, that he didn't understand what it meant. He says that next time he gets some money together he's going to cover it. He says he hopes I understand, and I do. I do understand being young and stupid. I do understand regret. I cross the room, I kiss him again, on the lips. The room dances around us and nothing is as important as our mouths, this heat, our bodies. I think I will get a tattoo, a bright red poppy on the small of my back, although I never do.

Tom can make anything happen. I watch his sleight of hand in awe. He balances potatoes and simmering onions in a pan, hands me a crisp orange carrot and pulls three more from behind his back. He performs for me in this little kitchenette and I am the captive audience, enchanted and eager for more, spellbound on the green couch in the tiny room on the top floor of the house. He is the cartoon snake and I am the girl with spirals for eyes. The air is filled with garlic and my throat is full of cheap dark wine. He kisses me and I am always falling, longing for the impact. That's the kind of power I believe he has. His roommates knock on the door, lured by the smell of the simmering stew and he turns them away. This meal is only for me. He doesn't need anything special, only the open throat, the cupboard of vegetables, the garlic on the windowsill, the suspension of disbelief. There is always one molecule, one tiny grain, the bursting seed in me that longs to be spellbound, bound, and offered up. He will find it. I will hand it to him, smiling.

The door bangs open and there is Tom, drunk, leaning against the doorframe. I have been awake for hours, sitting on the edge of the bed and drinking Jim Beam, wondering where he is. We were supposed to go see Malcolm's band together at the Albert. He was supposed to be home hours ago. I don't understand what is happening. *Where the fuck have you been?* I ask, anger clipping all the consonants. *Out,* he mumbles. *No shit,* I say. *Out where? We were supposed to go out together, remember? Where the fuck were you? Who were you with?* I know I'm raging but I can't seem to stop, my tongue is so loose in my mouth, my lips so tight. I'm standing in front of him. I can't stop yelling. *Shut up, you stupid bitch*, he yells. *I was fucking out, shut the fuck up!* His arm moves up from the side of his body, his hand tightens into a fist and swings out. It catches me across the side of my head and I fall to the floor. There is no breath left in my body and I'm as silent as granite. I hear the door slam again behind me and when I turn to look I'm alone again and the air is full of beer and whiskey and poison and my head throbs and the night has never been so long and empty.

Baby –

I can't face you. I'm so sorry. I don't know what to say to you except I'm sorry. That's not me, that wasn't me that hurt you, that was the person I used to be but I'm not that person anymore. I don't want to be that person anymore. There's this blackness inside of me and to tell you the truth it scares me and I need you so much, you're the one that's helped me to be different, to be better. You're the last person I ever want to hurt. I can't face it without you. Please give me another chance. You're so beautiful, you're too good for me, I don't deserve you, but I need you. I'll say it a million times, I'll do anything you want, I'll quit drinking, I'll go for counselling, whatever you say. Just please please don't leave me. I love you.

Tom

Tom –

I love you too. It's okay. I mean, it's not okay, but I understand. What you did was wrong, but I was out of line too. I understand about who you used to be and who you want to be. I believe in you. I'm angry and hurt but I'll get over it. What's important is us, that we keep trying, that we don't give up on each other. I'm not too good for you. We're what's good for each other, and we just have to keep remembering that. I believe you. And I need you too.

Let's give both of us a second chance.

I love you too.

xo

Carly tries to kill herself and I help her because I love her. I haven't slept for 48 hours because I've tried to leave Tom for the first time and he said he'd kill me. I run into Abby and she takes me home and we sit up and talk all night about what it was like before. Carly calls and makes me come over. Her roommates are out. She takes sleeping pills until she can't swallow anymore and then I crush them into a glass of water and she drinks and drinks and drinks. Carly is hallucinating and Elton John is singing, *Don't let the sun go down on me* but the sun is gone. The stars are smug and out of reach and I have to get Carly to the hospital because I don't want her to die. I don't know what I was thinking. One of her roommates comes home and we shove the wrong shoes on Carly's feet as we get her into the cab. The cabbie doesn't want to take us but I make him, and the nurse at the hospital doesn't want to deal with us but I make her. Carly asks her if she'd like a kitten or perhaps an anvil. I answer for Carly's medical history and they make her drink liquid charcoal. She throws up over and over again, all over herself, and doesn't understand why. She tells me about her grandfather's war medals and holds my hand and cries. Her roommate buys me coffee and tells me about his Gravol hallucinations and I don't care and I want to slap him. Her other roommate shows up. We used to be lovers and he holds me for a long time and I almost cry but I won't. I call my parents to tell them where I am and my mother shows up with Tom like she's doing me a favour and then I really do cry. They won't let me see Carly because she won't co-operate and then the emergency room fills up with hookers because a pimp got stabbed and everyone is sobbing and Tom is laughing and the walls fold inexorably inward. Carly is alone and confused and I am engulfed by rage and I helped her do it. The next day she tells the psychiatrist that she'll do it again and again. And so do I.

Winnipeg Times-Dispatch

TEEN SUICIDE RATE ON THE RISE

by Alex Podoluk

According to police, Winnipeg's teen suicide rate is on the rise for the second year in a row. Mandy Falks, a popular 17 year old high school student, jumped from the Provencher bridge early Sunday morning. People driving by witnessed the event and called police. Her body was recovered Sunday afternoon by police divers.

"Everybody loved Mandy. I didn't know there was anything wrong. I just don't understand," sobbed Alicia Emmonds, one of Mandy's friends. Her friends and family gathered on the bridge on Sunday afternoon, crying and throwing flowers into the river. Her parents, obviously distraught, declined to comment.

Mandy is the thirteenth Winnipeg teenager to commit suicide this year. Last year fifteen teenagers committed suicide, up dramatically from four the year before.

"We're not sure what the cause is," says Maryann Wilcox, director of Teen-Line, a Winnipeg telephone crisis line. "Certainly there are intense pressures on today's youth, including peer pressure on such issues as drug and alcohol use. Call-ins to our crisis line have also increased over the last couple of years. Youth are talking about problems such as teen pregnancy, drug abuse, and street life. We can hardly keep up with the demand," claims Wilcox.

Sources at the Health Sciences Centre say that there was another teen suicide attempt on the weekend. An unidentified teenage girl was admitted for a self-induced drug overdose. Doctors were able to intervene in time and the young woman was released on Sunday.

Statistics show that young women are more likely to commit suicide by overdose or drowning, while young men are more likely to attempt suicide by hanging or gunshot.

Carly runs out of money because she spent it all on the pills. She rents out her room in the duplex on Maryland, packs a backpack and her guitar and hitch-hikes to Vancouver with Dylan. They get chased by truckers, picked up by families and lonely people. She hates Vancouver. Some guy buys her a bus ticket back to Winnipeg but when she gets home she finds out her roommates have just finished a two-week party and the house is trashed. The landlord comes over and throws all her stuff into the back lane. We spend an afternoon picking through the alley for photographs, jewellery, clothes, records, anything not stolen or lying in a puddle. Someone's already been through it and there's not much left. We leave most of it for whoever comes along. We load everything into a shopping cart and push it five blocks to the Langside house, unload it in the room I share with Tom, a small heap in the corner. She'll sleep on the couch, or in the bed with me when Tom's gone out for the night and I don't know where he is. It's June and the sun casts a yellow sheen over our faces as we sit on the porch steps smoking cigarettes. She gets out her guitar and we sing a song that we wrote, something about loneliness and oranges. I find a half-full bottle of Jim Beam under the bed and it burns like knives and sunshine in our chests but we drink it anyway, between verses, singing as loud as we can to keep away endless Saturday afternoons in June, displacement, and loss.

Every morning we untwist our bodies from the sheets, bathe our thick tongues with water from the Jim Beam bottle beside the bed. The church isn't far away, and a motley group of us straggle from the house onto the slate-grey sidewalk and up the street. Carly and I sing, *If it's good enough for you / then it's good enough for me / to be a soup kitchen celebrity*. At the soup kitchen in the church basement there is:

stale bread
coffee
mysterious soup
day old doughnuts

Everyone smells bad, including us. It's hard to smell good in the summer. Sitting at the long tables there are:

old men high on sniff
young men high on sniff
a mom and her kids
tattooed, tattered, spike-haired us

Carly won't eat the mystery soup. She says she doesn't trust liquid food. She eats a whole tray of doughnuts while the nun tries to explain nutrition. Our bodies are brittle and indestructible. The trick to the soup is to dip the hard bread into it until the bread is soggy and all the broth has been absorbed. The other trick is not to think about all the other mouths that have closed around your spoon. The final trick is to be polite and pretend to pray. They might give you extra food, something to take home. We are assured that Jesus is smiling and I can't tell you how very happy that makes me.

Jeff's psychiatrist is easy with the prescriptions. There is always some pill or other under my tongue. I don't know their names or I can't remember them ten minutes later. Once Terry's entire body went rigid and I had to drag him to the hospital, hide his pet rats in the shoulder of my jacket. Once Jeff gave a handful to the girls from Balmoral Hall and we all almost got busted. There is always something going on. The pills lie in my palm like a rainbow. SNFU crashes from the second story window. Langside is the place to be, the street of riches. Sometimes the pills make Tom angry. Sometimes we both fall asleep and no one keeps track of how long we stay in our room. We wash them down with Old Stock and someone is always taking back the empties, buying cigarettes. We buy packages of noodles from the corner store, four for a dollar, and the old woman behind the counter counts out the dimes in slow motion. I count the tablets in my pocket and I have to keep starting over, one, two, red, blue, lavender, eleven.

Winnipeg Times-Dispatch

FUNDING CANCELLED FOR CORE AREA CRACKDOWN

by David Martens, Staff Writer

Winnipeg City Council has cancelled funding for year two of the Safe House initiative developed by the Core Can! organization. The program's goal was to identify substandard housing in the Core area, and to present City Council with a list of substandard properties and negligent landlords. "We're very disappointed that the funding has been pulled," says Safe House project co-ordinator Heather Wiens. "Our downtown neighbourhoods are overrun with dilapidated housing. This area has been the domain of irresponsible slum lords for too long." Wiens cites the recent fire at 154 Langside as an example of why Core Can!'s Safe House program is still needed. "That house was in terrible shape. It's lucky the whole block didn't go."

Friday's fire, which destroyed a rooming house at 154 Langside, is only the most recent in a series of Core area fires. Fire officials have not yet determined the cause of the blaze, although Wiens speculates that it may have been due to old and faulty wiring. The landlord of the property could not be reached for comment. No one was injured in the fire.

Last year in phase one of the project, Safe House conducted safety audits on homes and rental properties in the Core/West

Broadway area, in co-operation with homeowners and tenants. Phase two, scheduled for this year, aimed to work with the city and health and public safety departments to pressure slum lords to clean up decrepit properties. City Councillor for West Broadway, Markus Littleblood, said that he is also very disappointed by City Council's decision to pull Core Can!'s funding. "Perhaps my fellow councillors don't see West Broadway as a priority," stated Littleblood. "Perhaps they should spend some time here and see what terrible conditions area residents are forced to live in."

Core Can! will appeal Council's decision. Winnipeg mayor Sheldon Horotsky declined to comment.

HARGRAVE

Hargrave is the street where the skinheads live on the top floor, the chelseas one floor down. There is a never-ending supply of boots, cherry, black, oxblood. We tear the leather off the steel toes. This is a language that clears a path everywhere without moving our lips. This is where I learn about CSIS and police surveillance. Carly won't visit me. They take in some young punk and call him Igor and make him clean and cook, and there is always a girl around for a round of skull for the boys. My green and white and resilient blue body curls into a corner of the mattress on the floor and I spiral away on a silver thread of acid. Tom throws vodka into my eyes on New Year's Eve and I don't make any resolutions and I don't ask any questions and I don't don't don't.

We are in the new apartment on Hargrave and Tom's roommate is at work and we are deliciously alone. I have my blue guitar and Tom wants me to sing for him so I do, old songs and folk songs. I know my voice is terrible but he's smiling anyway and every time I stop he says, *No, sing me another one*. I am cross-legged on the floor cradling the guitar and he is sitting on the chair behind me, playing with my hair. I fiddle with the pegs, retuning, but Tom and I are in perfect tune with each other. I play a song that I wrote for him, another love song, and when I am done his voice is unsteady and he wraps his arms around me from behind and says, *No one's ever written me a song*, he says. *Thank you baby.* The afternoon sun gleams on the wood floors, puddles of gold, and I believe everything he tells me. I believe this afternoon will sustain us and last forever. My breath catches as he takes my guitar and leans it against the wall. He takes my hands and pulls me up, leads me into the bedroom and makes love to me on the mattress on the floor. Afterwards we share a cigarette and listen to the traffic, cars and horns and a siren. The day drips with music I can barely hear.

Winnipeg Times-Dispatch

GAY MEN FEAR FOR SAFETY ON DOWNTOWN STREETS

by Harrison Watkins, Staff Reporter

"This is the spot right here. You can still see the bloodstains on the concrete," says Rod McEllen, executive director of Operation Rainbow, Winnipeg's gay and lesbian resource centre. He is standing in a back lane just off Hargrave on a cool Monday morning, pointing to the spot where Wendell Hanks, 18, a gay male prostitute was savagely beaten late Saturday night. This past weekend witnessed at least three such assaults. "There may have been more," says McEllen. "Typically, gay men, especially prostitutes, are reluctant to report such crimes. We unfortunately do not have a good working relationship with the police."

According to McEllen, this Hargrave and Assiniboine alley is a little far from the traditional gay men's 'cruising' district, which is centred around the river walk closer to the Osborne Street bridge. "But the trade has been spreading out through downtown lately, mostly in response to the violence that was occurring on the river walk," claims McEllen. "Unfortunately, the violence seems to have followed."

Gay-bashings and other hate crimes, including the desecration of

Jewish cemeteries and synagogues, have been on the rise within the past year. The Hate Crimes division of the Winnipeg police currently have few leads on any of the recent spate of hate crimes, and are asking the public to come forward with any information they might have.

But McEllen says that gays and lesbians, and gay male prostitutes in particular, are unlikely to report most violent crimes. "In fact, many street workers claim that they have also suffered violence at the hands of the police. It's a dangerous world for them. Many young men have started carrying knives and other weapons. It's only a matter of time before the violence ends in homicide," concludes McEllen.

Police are advising all men to be cautious in the downtown area, especially at night.

Winnipeg
CITY OF WINNIPEG ENVIRONMENTAL HEALTH SERVICES
ORDERED
FOR INFORMATION REGARDING THIS ORDER CONTACT
CITY OF WINNIPEG ENVIRONMENTAL HEALTH SERVICES
986-2443

It is autumn in this city and the air feels sharp and dangerous in your throat, edged like promises, gilded like threats. The trees weep continuously, brittle orange and brown leaves that disintegrate under your boots. This city is consumed with thunder, it rains every night and the wet sky licks your face until you shine in the lightning. The wind in this city pulls at the zipper of your jacket and you take refuge inside a brick apartment building, listen impassively as the trees slap incessant distress signals against the windows. Something is going to happen, you feel the glinting edge of it in your chest. You close your mouth. You learn to wait.

Every time I descend the steep stairs into Wellington's I'm afraid that I'll fall. Down the stairs I can hear the trumpets of the ska band, and the stairs are crowded with skins and chelseas, smoking, talking, making out on the steps. I order two drafts, one for Tom, one for me. Tom lags behind me, stopping to talk every few feet. The pit is a green and black blur of boots and suspenders, white t-shirts and shiny scalps. I can feel the brass in the pit of my stomach and my neck is warm from the sour beery breath of the punk behind me. The rude boys are out, and the sharps, and the neo-Nazis. White and red and yellow laces stomp around me, and I am an invisible island. I see some girls that I know, there are always girls that I know although I'm never allowed to talk too much. I talk to them, a little, and I keep drinking draft. Later there will be a fight and I won't watch and I won't ask Tom what happened even after we leave and my ears will ring for two days with the promise of trombones.

I am in Simone's apartment at the other end of Hargrave, the big building with wide stone steps near the LC. Tom and her boyfriend Dermot hand us the acid, yellow mic, and then they leave, bigger better deals to make. Simone's baby is here with us, he is only a few months old and Simone is confident that she will know what to do. I don't believe her but I drop with her anyway. We wait until our bodies start to vibrate and the walls begin to breathe and then something is wrong with Simone and she edges to the bathroom to throw up over and over again while I smoke cigarettes and the baby sleeps. She won't stop throwing up and I have to concentrate very hard to hear what she is saying and I don't quite understand but the baby wakes up and I practice touching him. I practice dialing the phone but Dermot won't pick up his pager and won't call back. I don't remember how I get the baby into the carrier and onto my chest but I do and I'm so scared and the steps rise up to meet me as I creep down them. There are deadheads at Emma G's just up the block and they'll know what to do. The night is electric and all the leaves in the trees are dancing. I make it to the café and I have this tumor on my chest and I remember it is the baby. The guy behind the counter says, *What did you take?* and when I tell him yellow mic he says, *Well you know that I get all my acid from California* and I don't know what to say because I've forgotten. Some woman gives me ten dollars to take a cab to the hospital but after I've crept back to Simone's apartment and she's still throwing up she won't go because she's afraid they'll take the baby away if she shows up in the ER all fucked up on acid. Of course she's right and I light cigarette after cigarette, leave them all burning in the ashtrays. I must have put the baby back in his crib because there he is. Dermot and Tom must show up again sometime because I am at home again and Simone is not with me but I believe that I can still hear her thinking and the baby is crying and neither of us understands what it means.

Ashley is thirteen or fourteen, she dresses all in black and hangs out with her friend Jenn on the periphery of the skinhead circle on Hargrave. The skins aren't picky when they're drunk. One night I see her in the alley behind the apartment building, she's wedged between the garbage cans and crying. She says she's been raped. We all get raped. I tell her about Klinic and the rape crisis line, I tell her about the police but she says she won't report it. We never do. Her black eyeliner runs down her cheeks in watery streaks. I hold her and tell her she's beautiful and safe now. We all say the same things to each other, over and over again. She cries in huge gulps like a child. I only went out for a pack of cigarettes from the corner store, Tom is waiting for me inside the apartment and wondering where I am but at this moment I don't care. I call Ashley a cab and give her some money and settle her in the back seat, she leaves and I don't know where she's gone. Ten years later I will run into her in a subsidized housing building. She will remember me instantly but it will take me a few weeks to place her face because the story is familiar but there were just so many girls.

It is Christmas Eve and I shiver in my dress on the bus on the way to Tom's mother's house. She lives in Kildonan and that's three buses and at least an hour away but we promised that we'd come for dinner. When we get there Tom's older brother Sean grabs Tom around the neck and rubs his head and everyone is laughing. My dress has long sleeves but everyone assumes it's because of the cold and I laugh along, safe in this house. I drink a Coke, there is no alcohol in this house anymore and I am glad because I have seen Tom's secret scars, he has enumerated the stories of, *This is the time she pushed me down the stairs* and, *This is the time she locked me out*. Everyone tells the same stories but these ones belong to him and they break my heart. We have roast beef and Yorkshire pudding for dinner and it is so cold outside but this house is so warm. Tom's mother takes a picture of us eating cake for dessert and I smile and Tom makes a face and Sean rubs his full belly and the camera must be so full of light and love caught tight in the click of the shutter.

You forget that summer happens, you forget flowers craning up from the grass, you forget getting the mail barefoot, you forget naked arms. You forget sweat. You forget earthworms drowned in rain puddles. You forget rain. You forget making love without blankets. You forget kissing in the sun on a blanket. You forget fishnet stockings. You forget sunset after nine. You are a marionette controlled by the strings of your mittens. You sleep in flannelette and dream of wet wool. You forget that there is more than winter. You forget.

Tom is dazzling, he is as large as the façade of the burned out cathedral and there is a woman in the mirror who is silent and is not me. I am clothed all in purple like a morning glory and all the girls I meet are as silent as I am. It's simple, really. You just need to keep the girls from talking to each other, alone. You need to smash all the mirrors and leave only the rounded reflections of spoons. You kill the women by cutting them off from each other. Then we kill ourselves and you wash your hands, smooth and clean.

There are four of them, five of them, big men with shiny bald heads, the Ton of Fun club. They drink cases and cases of beer in a corner apartment on Hargrave, Screwdriver ranting incessantly in the background. I lie on the mattress on the floor in Tom's room and do homework, read *The Handmaid's Tale, Hamlet*, research the French Revolution. Everything is imbued with a sense of inevitability, doom, and I write frantically, fill notebook after notebook. They all go out drunk, come home drunker, their arms around each other's shoulders, singing, that old cliché. I don't want to know where they go but I do, I overhear them laughing about it later. I believe the phone is tapped and conspicuous men take pictures through the windows. Coming home on the bus one night I start to cry and a soldier from the base up the street asks me gently if I'm okay. The softness of his voice lodges in my own throat like a fist and I can't speak. He gets off the bus two stops before me and he's just another person that I never see again but never forget, this gallery of ghosts in my mind clamouring for help, immortality.

Tom shoves me into the hall and my arm is striped with purple lines like a barcode from his fingers. I hit the wall and fall in time to the Screwdriver refrain. I have no shoes and no jacket and nowhere else to go as Tom slams the door and locks it with a snap that reverberates in my ribcage. Michelle and Shauna live downstairs, the chelsea and the glam girl and I knock on their door, crying again, always crying without moving my lips. Shauna doesn't bother to ask what's wrong, the ceilings are thin and every girl's story blends into the next one. She says, *We're going out* and I say, stupidly, *I have no shoes*. She laughs and opens her closet and says, *What size are you?* There are mounds of boots, Docs, combats, black, blueberry, every colour. She gives me a pair of cherry 24-holes and my legs have never felt so lean, so ready to run. Michelle gives me fishnets and red lipstick and Dee-lite sings on the stereo *My succotash wish* and I am a shit-kicking princess in a miniskirt and flight jacket and I'm terrified that Tom will find out. We walk to the Spectrum and I can't remember who plays but I dance and drink screwdrivers all night, my own joke. It is dark and sweaty and the sound slams off the stone walls and I'm deep in the pit and I'm a blur of elbow and knee and I can't feel a thing and my body blossoms purple like an insomniac morning glory. Shauna and Michelle have my back and this night will never happen again. This freedom tastes like cocaine and it burns all the way down my throat. I get so strung-out that I can't remember how it ends but I know that Tom eventually opens the door and I'm not there.

ALBERT

Albert is the street of the bar and the streetwalkers huddled in Chopin's Café, a bullet hole in the blue stained glass of the door. We live in a room in the Royal Albert Arms and I hang my clothes on the exposed pipe bisecting the ceiling. There are rigs in every bathroom so I pee in the sink in our room. Bands play in the bar downstairs until 2 AM every night and the whole structure shakes and the thudding in my ears is sometimes blood and sometimes bass. NDI comes to town and it is a velour sex dance carnival. I listen to the radio play "Sweet Jane" and cry, missing Carly. The party always moves up to our room and I sleep through it all. I get up and go to work every morning as a telephone solicitor. No one wants what I am selling, only what they can take by force. I adopt a stray kitten. We are found out and kicked out on a hot day in July when the fire escape burns my hand.

Winnipeg Times-Dispatch

GAY-BASHING STRIKES TERROR

by Alison McKenna, Staff Writer

Skinheads are suspected in a vicious gay-bashing resulting in murder, Winnipeg police say.

Robert Michael Hawryluk was walking alone on the Assiniboine river trail behind the Legislative Building at approximately 11:30 PM Monday when he was viciously attacked and murdered. The river walk is a popular hangout for gay men and gay male prostitutes, and Winnipeg police are treating this case as a hate crime.

"It appears that Robert Michael Hawryluk was repeatedly kicked, and beaten with a chain and what appears to be a baseball bat," says Sgt. Doug Kilm. "His body was thrown into the river and stoned." Residents of a nearby apartment building called the police and an ambulance after hearing Hawryluk scream, but he was pronounced dead on the scene. Witnesses report seeing four men fleeing the scene.

Police suspect that these crimes may be linked to local skinheads. This is Winnipeg's twenty-fourth murder this year, and the fifth gay-bashing in the last month. Skinheads are suspects in the previous bashings. Police fear that the attacks are escalating, and plead with other witnesses and victims to come forward. "Bashings often go unreported," says Kilm. "If you know anything about these attacks, please contact the Winnipeg Police Hate Crimes Unit, or Crimestoppers. We need other victims to come forward and identify these men."

Hawryluk was a 24 year old man, originally from Swan River, who lived in an Assiniboine apartment and worked at Great West Life. Neighbours describe him as quiet and friendly. "He always had a smile for everyone," says neighbour Bill Kostas.

Police do not currently have any suspects in custody.

I listen to the radio late into the night, the CBC news every hour. They are warning people not to walk alone on Assiniboine behind the Legislative Buildings, especially young men. Young men turn up bloody all the time, it's getting more dangerous every day. Downstairs in the bar there's a fight every night except Sunday. There's always a switchblade or a broken bottle. One night Jenn throws a chair at her boyfriend. Danger loses its edge and it's hardly even a spectator sport. I flick the radio off, drop in a tape of Sarah Vaughan. Downstairs there's blood somewhere and I eventually fall asleep.

We own one plate, one bowl, three forks, one spoon, and a handful of blackened knives. We cook all our meals, illegally, in an electric frying pan, Kraft Dinner, noodles, fried potatoes, canned pasta in tomato sauce, nothing that needs a fridge because we don't have one. We eat bagfuls of soft white bread. The closest store is in the Bay, all the way up Portage at Memorial. We pile tins and boxes in my backpack because we aren't allowed food in our room, we can't be seen with it in the halls, carrying it up the elevator. I slip through these halls like a ghost, willing myself invisible. At night I dance alone in front of the window with the lights turned off, my hip bumping into the sink, singing *apple, banana, orange, green pepper*. The truck driver in the room next door bangs on the wall and the mirror shakes and my reflection trembles. I am filled with longing for water, for flesh.

Tom and I kneel together with a silver spoon bubbling over a lighter. My thumb blisters under the hot metal. Paint drifts from the walls in beige chips and splinters. Someone is thrown against the wall upstairs and the whole building shakes. I don't know where we get the rig from but it is pristine and hungry. I don't eat anymore but my heart is ravenous. Tom rips the filter off a cigarette and gently inserts the needle into the white cotton, dips the cotton in the liquid and slowly admits passage into the syringe. The filter keeps out chalk and slows the hardening of his veins. The insides of my arms are mapped with purple lines, pliant and submissive. I hold out my arm and it is not like an offering, not like a gift, it is only my arm. He ties me off. His thumbnail flicks against the glass as he knocks the air bubbles out. I make a fist, I remember this. He slides the needle in and he is gentler than any nurse, more accomplished than any lab tech, he has missed his calling or else he has found it here. The first wave of nausea doesn't overtake me, I am prepared, I have been warned. And then I am splayed and gridded by my veins, by the roll of gold and honey and I forget my tongue and Tom smiles and ties off his left arm right around the tattoo and takes three hits and one more was supposed to be mine and I've never wanted anything more but I can't talk and I can't move and I am the underwater seaweed that the schools of fish slip silently through, I am the pearl in the viscous mouth of the oyster and I remember that winter is over and I think, *I am molten snow*, I am the snowflake on fire and I want to kill him but I never do.

It is June and hot and I am sitting on the third floor fire escape at the Albert. I have a room but it is small and close and unknown odours seep from the curtains and the carpet and the bedspread. I know there's a maid because she stole my money from the drawer but I don't think that she cleans. There are buildings across the alley. There are windows in the buildings. I can see other lives behind the glass. There are bands jamming and artists silkscreening and someone is making tea. In the alley below me there is another fight. There is a crowd standing around in a circle. There is no one who sees me and the indigo sky tumbles around me like a river. The pavement is stained with blood and the bricks are tagged with graffiti and I draw hard on my cigarette, exhale grey smoke that drifts across the night and presses soft fingers against someone else's window.

Winnipeg Times-Dispatch

LETTERS TO THE EDITOR

Dear Editor,

This letter is in response to Morris White's Tuesday column ("Hand-out is a Hand-Up"). What a load of blarney. His advice represents soft-hearted liberalism of the worst kind. The worst thing you can do for these people is to give them money. Of course the woman that White spoke with is going to say that she uses the money to buy food. If she admitted that she's going to use it to buy drugs, alcohol, and cigarettes White never would have bought her lunch, never mind given her his supposedly hard-earned cash. I've worked hard all my life for my money. I got my first job when I was 12 and I never asked anybody for anything. Why can't these people get a job? It just makes me angry to see able-bodied people sitting on street corners asking decent citizens for money. Shame on you, Mr. White. You need to use tough love. If we all stopped handing over our cash these people would be forced to get up off their behinds and get jobs and stop being a drain on society.

—Alfred Sigurdson
Winnipeg

Summer lasts for years. We wade in the pond in Library Park until we're kicked out and then we lie in the grass and scare the secretaries eating bag lunches and reading novels. We wish we had bag lunches. Or pot. I'm sick of bannock. Bobby made bannock with drywall and ate it anyway because he was hungry and high, and he will always be known as Bobby Bannock. No one has a real name anyway, or they do and it's a legend, like Chris Peters, the oldest punk we know. We all hang out downtown, and we all panhandle. The pretty girls make the most. My long brown hair and Indian dresses guarantee me at least one bill among the change. We count the business men at lunch who won't make eye contact. It's a game, as good as any other. When they do meet my gaze their eyes are full of contempt or pity. Either one will do but I hate them together. If someone has a guitar we'll busk. You don't have to be good, just pathetic. Carly was busking on the ferry to Vancouver once and some guy liked her song so much he took her home and bought her a bus ticket to Winnipeg. Usually that story ends with rape but Carly is lucky. Today I am fairly lucky. I make enough for a pouch of tobacco and a gram. Tom takes the money. Tom takes everything, I know that by now. There's an outreach downtown where we can do our laundry for free so at least we don't smell bad. Everyone is golden and dangerous today. Every insult is extra funny. Every sip of whiskey from a communal pop bottle is extra raw. Everyone has a nickname and everyone knows what happened last night and everyone will be there again tonight and I am not alone.

Every second Wednesday is welfare day and I am filled with shame and loathing. Tom and I walk to the squat brown office on Broadway beside the Sal's, push the appointment slip and Tom's ID under the glass window facing the front doors. New cases to the right, standing appointments to the left. Once inside there is another glassed-in window to push our appointment card beneath. There are three open squares of chairs, blue, to sit on and wait for Tom's name to be called. No one calls my name, I'm legally his dependent, nothing is in my name but I'm required to show up to prove that I exist. I know we'll wait at least an hour longer than our appointed time, and I try not to catch anyone's eye. You'd be surprised at who you'll run into in the welfare office. Dermot's here, he deals and he's forgotten to turn his pager off. We turn to stare at him. Everyone knows that you've got to set it to vibrate before you walk in. The social workers are less concerned about the drugs than they are about the additional income. Everyone is very concerned about additional income. I hate it here and I'm bored and I'm scared to breathe too loudly. Never call attention to yourself. When Tom's name is called we sit in brown chairs in a cubicle, our backs facing the waiting area, while the social worker stares at us with watery eyes. He is tired and harassed, or she is suspicious and resentful. No one really expects to be treated well anyway. We have no income to declare, panhandling is untraceable. Tom tries to convince the worker that we need a new bed because you can't just ask for money, there are necessary codes: a new bed, winter jacket, property damaged by fire. There are strict regulations and it's all up to the whim of the worker. Today we get nothing extra. A baby wails in the background, it's been crying for over an hour and everyone is on edge. The worker hands us another slip of paper, we wait in another line for the cashier to give us the money. More glassed-in windows. Someone's drunk and smells, someone chases her kids. We have nothing and everything in common with each other but no one talks. Tom folds the money and puts it in his pocket, he gives me a five for a treat and I will spin that out like spider thread, secretly making it last another two weeks.

EVANSON

Evanson is the street where Tom and I move with the kitten. Tom collects fish in huge aquariums and beats me up, and I keep waiting for the floors to collapse under the weight of water. I call CFS on the neighbour and she calls a domestic on us. This is before zero tolerance and so I lie to the police again and again and they walk away empty-handed, are slower and slower to return. Carly inherits some money and spends it all and has nothing left so she comes to live with us. Tom hates her because he can't hit me while she's here and she hates him because she knows what he does and I hate all the hating and drink vodka straight. We make bannock and a tattoo gun, inscribe Carly's arm while we listen to John Prine. I cry alone in the dark the night before I have an abortion and Tom gets drunk with an old Langside friend and breaks all my glasses. No one sees my scars and Tom draws on all the pages in my journal so I'll always remember that he's watching.

It is October and I am shopping for a new blanket. I bled on the old one and I can't get the stains out, Rorschach blots of fear. *This one*, Tom says. *This blue one. It matches your eyes. You're so beautiful*. I am greedy. I lap up his words like milk in a saucer. *Really?* I say. *Really? You think I'm beautiful?* After the blood, I am always beautiful. I am charming and lovely and loved. Even standing in the middle of the aisle at Zeller's I am wanted and complimented and grateful. And secretly I'm proud of the fading yellow bruise on my cheek, I'm pleased because I know it sets off the azure of my eyes.

The walls are that particular shade of ecru that white paint becomes after too many cigarettes. I smoke too many cigarettes. It's hard to cry with a cigarette in your mouth. Inhale, hold, exhale, slowly. Breathe. Breathe. Tom punches another hole in the wall. There goes the damage deposit. Inhale. Breathe. I startle, now, at the ticking of the clock, loud as a gunshot in my ear. Exhale. Or I don't startle at all, I absorb everything into skin, tissue, the marrow of my bones. Yellowed flakes of paint settle into my hair and later I will wash them out in a scalding bath. Breathe. I even smoke cigarettes in the bath. Exhale. I walk around everywhere with holes in my memory and the taste of ashes in my mouth.

Some nights Tom gets so drunk that I have to push him home from the Albert on his skateboard. His flight jacket is orange inside, green outside, and is mottled with old specks of blood. I don't bother asking questions, Tom is past the point of speech and mumbles lines from MDC. All my curiosity has drained away. We steal ashtrays from the bar and they are hiding in my bag. We trace this pattern over and over again: up Albert, onto Portage, down Portage, up Evanson. Down Evanson, onto Portage, down Portage, onto Albert, glass rattling in my backpack. The skateboard wheels rattle over small pebbles and the buses have stopped running hours ago. There's only money for a cab on cheque days, and even then Tom would rather spend it at the bar. The walk clears my head and I only stumble occasionally. Tom never falls. He is always in control even when out of it, his muscles coiled, his legs balanced. My legs are ready to run, ready to curl around my body, knees to forehead. The board sags in the middle, the night sky leans onto my back, and the occasional car drives by and blares the horn but they never stop and neither do I, steady as a heartbeat.

I am newly pregnant and slightly rounded, I have begun to eat apples voraciously. I throw them up over and over again in Klinic's clean white bathroom. My belly has become fecund. Above my head there are birds flying south and stars explode from my throat when I speak. Something large and soft has taken over my body and a pearl grows inside of me. I don't want this, I can't do this, and this is easy to fix. Tom hates me for my decision, he keeps me waiting for an hour at the Women's Pavilion, he makes me ask my parents for cab money, and he goes to his friend's house to play Dungeons & Dragons when it's all over. I lie on the carpet curled like an empty husk around a pillow, shaking and bleeding. I can't protect anything.

Pregnancy Counselling Clinic

Laminaria Tent Insertion
____________________.Women's OPD.

Surgery _________________________

Please report to the Admitting Office,

Main Floor
Women's Hospital
735 Notre Dame Avenue,
Winnipeg

2 hours before your surgery time

If for any reason you change your mind regarding your Surgery or your Laminaria Tent Insertion, please call 555-3980 at least 48 hours in advance to let us know.

Sunlight settles in pools in all the leaves, and the pavement is sticky with aphid shit. Carly lives in the basement of a house, eats crackers at a soda table and watches horror movies, sitting on couch cushions on the floor. She is as pale as calla lilies, her transparent skin as smooth as coffin linings. She leaves the house once every two days to walk over the bridge to the movie store in the Village and back, head down, striped pyjamas striding. I visit her all summer, we pass a bottle of sambuca between us and fill our minds with murder, monsters, midgets and knives. She names her plant Dario Argento, becomes obsessed, writes him letters, learns Italian. I talk and talk but she doesn't hear me. I wear long sleeves to hide the bruises, my arms are spotted and smudged like star lilies but it is cool in the basement and she doesn't notice. I am afraid that one day she'll start walking and keep going, that I won't have anywhere to go and she won't be anywhere at all.

I make pale yellow cookies with pink icing. I live in the apartment with Tom and the fish and the budgies, blue, yellow, purple, green. I need something to take care of. It's early Sunday morning and we have just come home from the vet's. I woke up this morning to screaming. One of the pet rats had caught a budgie's leg and was chewing it off. Rats have very strong teeth, yellow and sharp. I didn't know that birds could make such a sound. The vet said it wouldn't live through an amputation and so we put it to sleep and now we owe another sixty dollars. I carry the carcass home and wrap it in pink satin, put it in the freezer to wait until the ground thaws. The rat has cleaned all the blood away from her mouth. Rats are very clean animals. I pick her up, gently, in my hands, and quickly snap her neck. Once they have the taste for blood you can never trust them again. I wrap her in blue velvet and put her in the freezer beside the dead budgie. I spend the rest of the day baking sugar cookies, stirring icing, sweet enough to rot your teeth.

IF NOT CALLED FOR, RETURN TO
Jeffrey Dean Marks
P.O. Box 130
Headingly Jail
Headingly, Manitoba
ROH OJO

A Heathen's work is never done –

In the name of Death, War, Famine, And Pestilence... Greetings. It is I, Heathen X, Jeff of the Apocalypse. Bow down, tell all. First of all, I'm addressing this letter to you, since Tom, you cheap son of a bitch, can't even spend 47 cents on a stamp to mail me a fucking letter. I'll remember this. I'll make your dough-boy ass pay when I get out of here. I tossed in a couple of extra stamps in case you want to mail me a second letter. Since Tom, that useless excuse for an evolved man, probably eats away all your hard earned money. This is just a short letter. I don't feel much like writing letters right now. I'll write you a real one after I get another one from you (although I suspect that you will be doing most of the writing since "YOU TOM" can barely put together a sentence speaking, never mind putting it down in writing!). Tom, if you can't tell, I'm trying to make up for all the insults I've missed giving to you the past few months.

As for you going back to school, some people will never learn. As for Tom going back to school, I think the novelty will wear off in a couple of weeks and he'll be back doing what he does best, which is nothing! However, I could be wrong. Could be that he'll never make it there in the first place. At the moment, not a hell of a lot is new with me. Next week I get the results of my G.E.D. Soon I'll be putting in for a T.A. to a half-way house. Less than a hundred days of rest and rehabilitation to go! And being myself always provides me with entertainment. There's a rumour going around the guards that I'm a Satanist. They won't even let me work in the kitchen. Fucking screws. They also think I've tried to recruit a cop's daughter!! It's true that I've been communicating with a cop's daughter, but the rest is all just a misunderstanding. The cop saw one of my letters and punched my name into the computer. Needless to say, he wasn't very impressed. He called the administration here and complained about me talking with his daughter. Anyway, one of the top guards calls me into his office and tells me that communication with this girl has got to "CEASE RIGHT THIS INSTANT" or I get my phone privileges taken away, which means getting stuck in the hole for the rest of my bit. Oh well, that's how that rumour started. Quite a few of the guards are really freaked out having a "Satanist" around, or so I'm told by another of the top guards. Oh me, I'm such a victim. Those bastards did one fucking major search on my cell tonight. They spent half an hour ripping it apart. Fuck does it piss me off when they do that!! Alas, the life of an institutional inmate. I'm expecting some god-fearing guards to come and pull me out of my cell in the middle of the night and try to beat the so-called devil out of me. The price I pay to amuse myself, I wonder if it's worth it? Of course it is, shit! Even if it cost me some extra time I'll do anything to amuse myself. I'll never learn my lesson?!

I'm going to sign off. Tom you fat bastard, take care of your woman or she'll kick your ass. I'll be out pretty soon to kick your ass myself. You, my dear, send me some more letters. Please?! That's enough for now. Until I hear from you again or until I'm released, Dig Ya,

Heathen X

HOME

Home Street is where I live when I leave Tom and move in again with Carly. She borrows clothes from the costume store where she works and we dress like old movie stars and promise each other we'll never leave. Of course Tom eventually moves back in. I drink PCP tea out of translucent china to turn my life into a poem and it almost works and I almost erase myself like a mistaken metaphor. I have an affair with the working girl two floors down. We kiss while we wait for her phone call and her driver. I wait for her to shower when she comes home again while her little girl sleeps. The caretaker is a man who'd killed his social worker with a hammer when he was fourteen and had already served his time. We get into an argument in the hallway and he calls me a bitch and Tom and I move out and Carly moves to Vancouver and I never see my girlfriend again, although I hear that her boyfriend pushes her down the stairs and she loses her baby. One story is very like another.

Tom lives in a house on Home Street with Derek and Kevin. GWAR and Black Flag and DOA are the sound-track backdrop to every conversation. Not that anyone talks very much. Every night there's another reason to drink hard. I cross Portage and walk the three blocks to the house because Tom wants me to. One night they throw a shopping cart out of the second story window as I unlatch the gate. Next to go is an aquarium and the grass is strewn with glass shards like sharp transparent poison flowers. There are no flowers, not even dande-lions. Upstairs I find Tom in bed with Melanie. She plays the bass and just moved to Winnipeg from Gimli and Tom can't resist a virgin. He sees me seeing him and then all those terrible things start to happen again. He tells me:

Get the fuck out.
Don't come the fuck back.
You stupid fucking bitch, I'll fucking kill you if you show your fucking face here again.

I look at Melanie and she looks at me and licks her lips. I turn and run down the stairs and through the glass and out the gate and up the street. My phone is ringing when I get home and my shredded chest burns inside with shards of fire. Derek's voice is like velvet on the other end of the phone. He says:

Come back.
It's my house too.

I want you here, I'll protect you, don't be afraid.

I know he's drunk and he's no match for Tom and I know that he doesn't want me, only parts of me:

My breasts
My mouth
My cunt

But I want I want I want someone to fall into and I know he'd catch me for at least an hour or two but I also know that I'll catch it later if I go and so I don't. I sit cross-legged on my bed and listen to Billie Holiday sing, *Oh my man, I love him so / he'll never know* and I don't answer the phone again until the sun rises in gasps of pink and shreds of orange and the flowers in the park across the street open all their hungry mouths.

Baby –

I'm sorry about yesterday. I know I've said this before, but it won't happen again. But you've got to help me. We've both got to try harder. You've got to try harder not to make me angry. I just get so angry and it's like blackness all around me and I don't know what I've done, I don't know what I'm doing. I love you so much. I don't want to be angry at you. Sometimes I think you make me angry on purpose and I don't know why you'd do that but don't you see that nothing good happens when I'm angry, it's all bad. I'm bad, I know that. I need you to make me good. I can't do it without you. Please understand.

Tom-Tom

Carly –

I just can't handle anything right now. People say, "How're you doing?" and I'm stuck. I have absolutely no idea what to say. So obviously I'm not doing okay. There's something big and black and scary inside of me that I need to figure out. So please don't be offended, but I'm not leaving my room or talking to anyone until I understand what's going on. I'm not mad at you, but I can't talk to you. I hope you understand. I don't think I'm making much sense. Maybe I'll come out at night to eat. Maybe I'll come out in a couple of days or maybe longer. I don't know, but please be patient with me, and please keep loving me. I love you.

xo

Hey –

Good luck on your not-yet-mid-life-crisis. I'm not mad at you. Do whatever you need to do. I'll be waiting. Maybe I'll slide a pop-tart under your door. Don't die. Come back to me. Gimme gimme shock treatment. I'll let you have Froot Loops when you get out. Love you.

Your crazy insane roommate,
Carly

Carly is moving to Vancouver. Her friends have just gotten married and they're driving west with a trailer hitched to the back of their car and Carly hitches a ride with them. Carly and I once wrote a song for a friend of ours when she left and it goes, *You go out west to find yourself but it's all been done before* and it plays over and over again in my mind. Carly packs her clothes and her Star Wars toys and her hundreds of videos, sells the sofa and the TV, leaves me the coffee table. She leaves me on a sunny day in August while all the snapdragons tremble and long for the pinch of my fingers to open their pink and lavender throats. Carly hugs me and her apartment keys jingle behind my back, she hands them to me and steps off the curb and is swallowed up by the blue car. Tom is watching from an upstairs window. They have nothing to say to each other. *I love you* she said, I said. *Don't*, I want to say, *don't don't go*, but the car is already driving up the street past the park. It pauses briefly at the stop sign, waits for an opening, and then turns onto Portage, lost in the traffic, heading west.

Baby –

I don't know why I do this. I want to stop but I don't know how. If I don't stop I'm going to die. I don't want to die. I don't want to leave you. I love you more than anything and I'm sorry sorry sorry sorry sorry sorry sorry sorry sorry doesn't take it away please take it away the blackness is closing in again I don't know what to do I don't know how to stop it stop it stop it stop it stop it stop it stop it stop it stop it I know need help I need you to help me.

Help help help help help help help help help help help help help help help
help

Love love love love love love love love love love love love love love love love

Tom-Tom

I finally go back to high school, Argyle, a school where I don't have to show up if I have a black eye, a split lip. They let you graduate no matter what your attendance is. Tom stays home and drinks and paints miniature models of warriors. A famous journalist from Toronto is the guest of honour at our graduation. She works with AIDS hospices and women's shelters and when she signs my book my eyes burn and I think, *Take me with you*. And then I think, *I don't deserve to go*. There is no self-pity, only fact. I have done nothing to merit extraordinary measures of kindness. Something weighs heavy and muddy at the edge of my mind but I push it away. My science teacher gives me a rose and I cry. At home I hang it upside down from the kitchen doorway, try to preserve it, but it turns brown and crisp and one day I bump into it by accident and it crumbles in papery flakes on my shoulder. I put my diploma away in a box and wonder what I should do next.

I long for textbooks, fat with creamy pages and dense with small black words, classrooms crowded with tables and orange plastic chairs, reams of paper blank and lined in blue. There is no money for university. I take a job as a cashier at the local grocery store, where my long brown braid and white shirt with tiny flowers convince my new bosses and the customers that I am lovely, sweet, and untouched. I am hopeless, and the other girls are very patient. They show me over and over again how to change the roll of receipt paper in my till, how to subtract mistakes that I've miskeyed, how to carry a full pail of soapy water up the stairs without spilling. On my first night shift my boss hits on me while I'm mopping the floor and my cheeks burn and someone has stolen my tongue. Every morning I stand at my counter and clip the date out of yesterday's unsold newspapers, read the headlines and absent-mindedly wipe newsprint across my face. There is a new murder every week or so, a new bloody corpse discovered under a bush, behind a building, a press conference called by the police, a photo of the chief looking competent and concerned for the camera. There is a secret world behind the newsprint and I tie my apron tighter around my waist, scissors gleaming, my mind blank as a page.

I have just come from Klinic where the doctor told me that I'm pregnant as I sat in the brown chair and cried. The nurse set up an ultrasound appointment and of course I know what my options are. I am at home staring out the window at the snow-covered swing set in the park and Tom is not here. I don't know where he is but I assume he'll turn up. I turn to stare at my reflection in the mirror. I stare back at myself, blotchy and blurred around the edges. I place my hand on my belly and I can't feel anything. It is two weeks before Christmas and I haven't had any money to buy presents yet. I think that this small thing growing inside me is a gift I do not deserve. I think, *what can I offer this child?* I will keep this child and she will be strong and fierce, stronger than me, fiercer than me. She is already tenacious, burrowing and clinging to something deep inside of me. I will not tell anyone yet, not even Tom, and sitting on the edge of the bed in this wood-edged room I realize I'm no longer alone.

I met Zava at Argyle, the alternative high school filled with moms and drop-outs and freaks and lonely people. We become lovers one night at her house on Young street but Tom doesn't know. Zava and I sit on the blue couch on the third floor on Sunday mornings and smoke joints, listen to Arlo Guthrie, hold hands and watch the still blue sky out of the streaky window. After Carly moves away Zava and I hang out at her place on Lipton, drink herbal tea out of a teapot shaped like an orange and gold elephant. She knows about Tom but we don't talk about it. At night we go to the Albert, all of us, me and Tom and Zava and her boyfriend Ted. They drop tiny white perfect panes of acid and my belly stretches swollen in front of me. At the bar, Zava stands with her arms crossed between me and the pit, shoves back anyone who gets too close. I can't remember the names of all the bands we see but I remember Zava's crossed arms, her straight back, the way she leaned into my belly like a caress, and everything she shielded me from while she could.

I am pregnant and I crave lemons, vitamin deficiency. On my break at the grocery store I pick lemons out of the produce shelves, cut them into wedges and suck the juice through my teeth, squinting my eyes, relishing the tart burn on the sides of my tongue. I stare at the yellow rind and think sunshine, gin, penicillin, tea. The baby lifts her elbow or her knee and I can see the sudden bulge in my belly. Three more hours until I go home and I stretch the minutes out, spray and wipe my counter over and over again. Tom is at home playing death games on the computer, waiting for me to come back. It's payday and I cash my cheque at the store, it's the only way I'll ever see the money. I buy armfuls of fruit on my way home because Tom can't take them back, they're mine. Lemons, kiwis, apples, strawberries, plums, and twenty dollars in my pocket that I won't tell Tom about. When I get home Tom demands the money and I give it to him, I'm too tired to argue, but he never asks to see my pay stub and he doesn't know about my nest egg, sweet and sharp and hidden deep in my pocket.

I've just finished an eight-hour shift at the grocery store. The baby has shifted and lifted her leg, her arm, inside me. I've counted nickels and pennies and coupons and seconds. I've mopped and stocked and smiled smiled smiled at every customer. I've punched in codes for asparagus (24), a 5 lb bag of Yukon Gold potatoes (114), English cucumber (36). The girls told me on my first day that banana (11) is the first one you learn, the one you never forget: urban legend, cashier code, numeric nightmares.

I've just finished an eight-hour shift and I'm tired deep inside my cartilage, the roots of my hair. My fingernails are rimmed with coin dirt and ache for sleep. I open the apartment door and Tom has the guys over, five men with blue mohawks and black dreads and shiny scalps and beer and Wild Turkey. In the bedroom, behind the French doors, I start to cry again, all I do is cry, oceans of salt, pillars of stone. Of course I am too loud. Tom comes in because I'm embarrassing him in front of his friends. His hands close around my neck:

(this is the code to shut up)

He cracks my head back against the headboard and I cross my arms over my belly

(this is the code to protect the baby)

I say no no no no no no no no no and he releases my throat and punches my nose and I start to bleed and bleed and my white work shirt is covered with blood like salty jam, like a miscarriage, like a murder.

(this is the code to stop talking stop weeping stop stop stop)

The pain rolls through my body like thunder and for once I scream and all those men on the other side of the door don't hear me. Or maybe they do because I hear them all laughing. Sometimes it's hard to tell who knows what and who cares. Tom leaves and gently slides the door behind him and I hold tissue against my nose and I'm too afraid to cry and the baby turns inside me and all I can see are bananas turned crimson and all I can think, stupidly, is code red, code dead,

(11)
(11)
(11)

Carly lives in Vancouver in a house full of hippies who walk around barefoot and won't let her keep meat in the fridge. She moves into another house, and then another. My address book is full of crossed out numbers. She gets into a fight with the friends she drove out with and doesn't see them anymore. She cries on the phone and tells me she hates it and I tell her to come home but she won't. It's always raining out there when we talk, I can hear it in the background, sliding down the glass and pooling on the sidewalks. I tell her about the baby perched precariously inside me, the bile that lurches from my throat every morning. She asks me to promise to make her the godmother and I don't believe in god but I promise anyway, anything to keep her on the line, to keep her in my line of sight. My phone bill is outrageous and I can't afford this friendship but I do anyway. She doesn't ask about Tom and I don't tell her. *Remember that night*, I say, *remember that night when I tried to set you up with Kevin and we had him over for dinner and I burned the rice and the smoke detector went off and we all had to stand on the fire escape until the air cleared?*

I remember, she says. *I remember that he was a nice guy but he was a racist skinhead.*

He is, I say.

He still is, or he's a punk or he's just some guy who means well but doesn't know any better or he does and he doesn't care. It just didn't seem so important at the time.

Okay, I say. *Okay, remember that other time?*

Derek is going to be a piercer. One day he will own his own shop, he will lobby for health code regulations, his name will be in all the papers. But not yet. Tonight we are in Zava's living room with her boyfriend and her roommate and my shirt is off and Agnostic Front is screaming, *Everybody's got a price to pay / It's my it's my it's my life* out of the stereo. My adrenalin thuds in time to the bass. Derek has clamps and a hollow needle and a blue ring with a black ball, I watched him sterilize them on the stove in the kitchen and he's going to pierce my nipple. Zava holds my hand as Derek adjusts the clamp. All the blood has to drain away and I gasp and practice breathing from the top of my chest. I sit on the yellow couch, clamped, for five minutes or two weeks. Zava plays with my hair, it is long and straight and brown and she braids and unbraids it, her fingers like snakes. I try not to move. And then Derek says, *Ready?* and pushes the needle through. It is sharp and silver and scores a hole through my flesh. I breathe. I breathe. He says, *Ready?* again and attaches the ring to the end of the needle and pulls the whole thing through and Agnostic Front is still screaming and I am not. Zava's boyfriend turns green and tastes bile and has to leave the room. Derek uses pliers to pull the ring into the little black ball and I have never felt pain like this or I have but this time I choose it. I choose it and I am beautiful and Zava kneads her fingers deep into my shoulders and her boyfriend comes back with some PCP and I take a line, I take another and I am floating away from the pain. I can't touch myself or put my shirt back on and Derek gives me a bottle of witch hazel and I did it I took it all and no one can say that I'm weak, that I can't take it, that I can't take anything. I answered yes yes yes and I carry the weight of this black little world on a shining ring and I can take anything you've got to give.

RUBY

Ruby Street is where the police show up one May afternoon to take Tom downtown to the PSB and they won't tell me why, but want me to search through all my old journals for a particular date. I try to explain that all my journals are tainted and I don't have what they want and I decide not to let Tom come back. He comes back anyway and shows me his gun, but when the police come back I look and look and can't find it. I cry on the phone to Carly and the crisis shelter and learn words like Non-Mol and remember names like Wodin's Front. I cut off all my hair and have an affair with a soldier. The walls are covered in white and gold velvet and I learn to lock all the doors all the time and I taste freedom with the pink tip of my eager tongue and I keep moving.

Tom and I live in a rooming house here. There is no phone jack but there is a payphone beside the laundromat on Westminster. I keep a roll of quarters to hold inside my fist at the bar and I break into it periodically to make outgoing calls. *Oh sure, I'm fine. What about you? We're going out tonight. Will you be there?* We are always going out. Everyone is always there. One night I lose the key to the padlock on our door. Tom has to borrow an axe from the neighbour who collects crossbows. He breaks into our room and then he breaks into me because it is always my fault. It is always raining this summer and there are always streaks of tears on the window. Someone steals our food out of the fridge and I remember that ownership is all in the mind. I don't need food anyway when I'm so full of love and silver quarters like wafers.

It is six o'clock in the morning on a new day in July, sticky and hot, and I awaken in a pool of amniotic fluid, contractions, as they say, wracking my body. At the hospital there is no relief, only this pain, and I slowly walk up and down the tiny park beside the river, willing the child to come. Tom wants to take a nap in my hospital bed, he won't get out even when I yell at him. I finally send him home. He turns up later with his mother and I hate them both and they finally leave again. The baby will not come, she is waiting for something. I am waiting to die but I know that I won't. There is no melodrama, only pain. She finally kicks and claws her way out of my body at six o'clock the next morning and I am so exhausted that I cry and I don't know what to do with her. She lies on my belly, sticky and wet, and she is of course miraculous, she is of course perfect, but I'm just so very tired.

The baby has finally been born, a small wrinkled girl child. She sleeps in a bassinet at the foot of my hospital bed while the woman in the bed next to mine cries softly. Zava comes to visit me and brings her daughter Lucy, she plays with plastic blocks on a blanket on the floor. I haven't named my baby yet, there is power and destiny in a name and I need it to be perfect. I'm so tired and sore that I can't sit up very well, I can hardly feed myself but I know I have to, there's this small life that needs me and I have to be ready, I have to be competent, I have to be more. Zava gently strokes my hair with a soft brush and I'm so grateful. Tom hasn't come to visit me. I know he wanted this baby and I don't know where he is and I don't understand. The payphone is at the end of the hallway and that feels like miles away. I had this vision of flowers and balloons and stuffed animals littering my bare bedside table and I feel so foolish. They serve fish for dinner and I hate it and can't eat it and I feed it to Lucy in little pieces. Zava finally has to leave as the bright evening sun pierces the window, but she promises she'll be back tomorrow. She brings me the baby and I settle her in my awkward arms, prepare to try to learn again how to breast feed. A nurse pops her head in the door every few hours as the room slowly darkens. The baby starts to cry again and I can't make her stop and I don't know what to do and the night stretches black and interminable in front of me.

I don't have money for a birth certificate, they make you pay, even for a brand new life. I grip the pen tightly and carefully form the letters on the live birth registry, the only identification I'll have for her: Maiia Carly. It's taken me three days to come up with the right name, the perfect name. In an hour I'll take her home in a taxi and she'll be all mine, Tom and I will be all alone with her. A nurse will make a home visit in a week ostensibly to offer help but I know she'll be checking up on us, surveying my home, my ability to parent. I'll have to find time to clean. I'll have to find the energy to get out of this hospital bed, put clothes on, take Maiia in my arms and walk downstairs. I'll have to find the strength to bring her home, to say the word *home* and mean it. I'll have to find a way.

Zava and her boyfriend have broken up. She's had enough of him cheating on her, the endless denials, the pitying looks of her friends. Zava is not a woman to be pitied. She has an aunt in Toronto, she's going to go east and apprentice at a tattoo shop, she's going to drive beauty and rage and colour into people's skins. They are going to pay her for it. Her aunt is going to watch Lucy during the day, it's all arranged. She'll leave the long distance charges for Ted to pay. Lucy crawls around on the floor while I hold Maiia on my lap. This apartment suddenly seems impermanent. The walls are drywall illusions held together with paint and wishing. I wish Zava would stay. I wish I could go with her. I can't go, her aunt doesn't have room for all of us. And how can I leave? Zava gives me her aunt's phone number, it only takes her a few hours to pack while I keep Lucy busy, feeding her Cheerios and homemade applesauce. Zava gives me the elephant teapot, we both cry, but I can see how excited she is by this new life opening up in front of her. I'm so jealous and scared that I feel sick. By the time Ted gets home they'll be gone and he'll get angry and yell and maybe cry but it won't matter, it won't change anything, Zava and Lucy will be on a bus eating crackers and cheese and he won't know where they are and I'll never never tell.

Tom rapes me one night as Billie Holiday sings softly to me in the background. *It ain't nobody's business if I do.* I know how the song goes and I think *this, again.* Tom says it's been long enough since the baby was born and he has needs and rights. I don't know what's right. I know this isn't right but Tom won't listen. My body screams *no* but I listen to the music and I hold my breath and I try to float away and I submit.

Tom has locked himself in the bathroom and he is crying and he says he is going to kill himself. We are like one person. He knows what I'm thinking before I say it and he tells me everything, everything. We sleep together, we eat together when we eat, he tells me what I need to do and I tell him when I need to do it. When he cries late at night tears collect in the corners of my eyes and I hold him or he holds me and there is nothing else in the world. I am crying right now and Maiia is crying and Tom is crying too, I can hear him through the door, heaving sobs from the bottom of his stomach. I know he doesn't know how else to say I'm sorry and I know that it will all be my fault for not forgiving him, for not being more understanding, and I think, *What kind of person am I?* I know that if the sound stops on the other side of the door I will drop down dead as a stone and it's always all my fault.

There are always pauses, moments of infinite tenderness and faith, the times when I turn to Tom and there is no one else in the world, skin to skin. I'd like to say that I only stay because of terror but within the fear there are deep pools of love and I keep falling in. I keep kissing the beast and I alone am the witness to the torment behind his eyes. I wake up every morning and think, *Wake up, wake up, transform, I'm waiting*. I know what that story's really about but I believe it anyway.

Tuesday and Wednesday mornings I take Maiia downstairs to our neighbour, Robyn. I leave her milk in bottles, blankets, toys, and I take the bus to the university to learn about crises of faith in the modern era. Tom stays upstairs and takes the computer apart and puts it back together again, obsessively wiping the hard drive, reformatting, rebooting. I don't trust him with the baby. He loves her but he forgets to change her, doesn't understand what to do when she cries. Sometimes I don't understand what to do either and I cry in fatigue and fear. I don't sleep very much. I sit up with Maiia late at night watching talk shows while Tom is out with his friends. He comes home and passes out in bed and I sit up until dawn, rocking back and forth, back and forth with the baby. Sometimes he lifts her way up in the air above his head, swings her around, and I watch with my breath tangled and knotted in my throat. He is not quite careful with her, he tries but I don't believe he understands just how easily she breaks. I am broken in a million different secret places and I'm too tired to put myself together again. Robyn brings me muffins and my heart breaks with gratitude. I eat them one-handed, holding the baby, always holding the baby with the other arm. Tom rarely holds the baby. He says he doesn't know how and I scream at him, *How the fuck am I supposed to know? Like this, like this, figure it out.* I think I do my best but I don't know how good that is. I start to cry again in rage and despair and Maiia starts to wail again so loud that I can't even hear Tom slam the door again on his way out.

The police are at my door except they don't look like police, they're dressed in suits like Amway salesmen or Mormons. They're extremely courteous and something soft and cold rolls over in my belly. They take Tom away for over twenty-four hours and when he comes home he is grey and his eyes are red and he starts crying. *It wasn't me,* he says. *I don't remember, it wasn't me.* I don't know what he's talking about. I know I should comfort him but something rolls over in the corner of my mind and I don't want to touch him. *What did they say?* I ask. *Where were you? Why didn't you call? I tried calling the police, the PSB, the Remand Centre, but no one would tell me anything. I didn't know what to do.* I don't know what to do now, watching Tom sob at the kitchen table. Something is wrong, something is wrong, and then the baby starts to howl too and outside spring is trying to pull itself up the icy banks of winter and I'm afraid to leave the house and I don't understand why.

Everyone knows you never tell a crisis line that you have a gun but you did it anyway and I guess it was some kind of textbook cry for help but you can cry somewhere else and then oh then the police showed up five or six of them and I was sleeping with the baby and they were breaking in the door and I didn't know what was happening and they searched the house like a dark blue nightmare and of course there was no gun or there was but you'd left it with someone else for safekeeping and the officer in charge kept asking me if there was anything I wanted to tell him while you waited in the back of the squad car in the lane and I foolishly said no and no and I just didn't know that he was offering to help because he couldn't say it just like I couldn't ask for it. And then they made you give me half the money and they drove you to your friend's place for the night and there was nothing nothing to stop you from coming back and so you did you did you did.

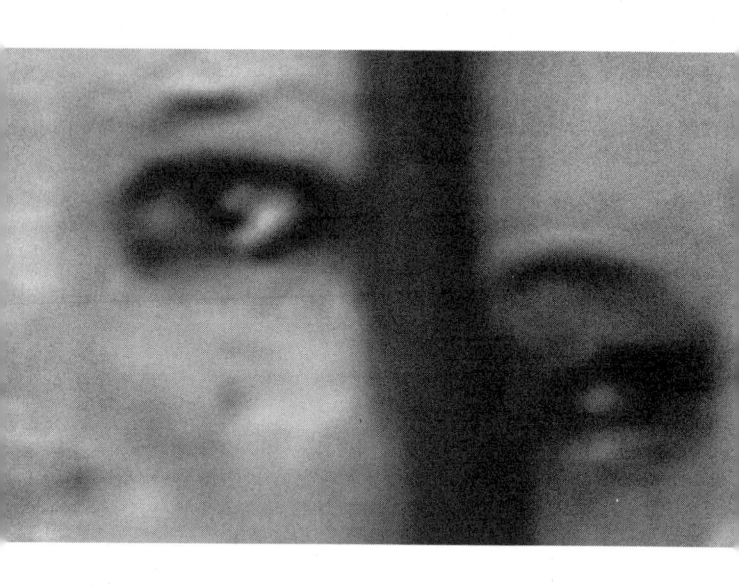

Carly's back for a visit. She and I sit in a blues bar on Main Street. It is two in the morning and I have never felt more awake. *I think it's time,* I say. *I don't want to do this anymore.* I am drinking but lucid. Across the table Carly leans forward. *Whatever you need to do,* she says. She is calm but elated. I take a long sip of my beer and let the steel guitar slide against the insides of my ribs. I am terrified but I have never felt more sure. Tom is at home with Maiia. When I get home I will sit at the kitchen table while he demands to know what's wrong. I will refuse to tell him but he will insist and the words will leak from between my lips and I will be a river full of rage and fury but I will never have been more centered. He will stay the night but in the morning I will make him leave. I will never let him come back and between my ribs a small worm grows and it wriggles even while I'm sleeping and I name it *hope.*

I sit in a blue plastic chair, in a row of other blue plastic chairs, in the downtown Greyhound bus terminal. Maiia is in my arms, sleeping, the delicate blue veins in her eyelids quivering. Tom doesn't know it but I've been saving money, scraps here and there, a Christmas cheque from my father that he doesn't know about, all carefully secreted in a bus depot locker. Outside, the gaping bellies of busses are being stuffed with knapsacks and suitcases, long green rolls of army duffle bags. I have two small bags that I also keep in a locker here, they've been waiting in this dark metallic cave for a month. I visit them when I can slip away. Tom doesn't know where we are, he thinks we're at the library. It takes over fifty hours to drive to Vancouver, across the interminable prairies, through the undulations of Alberta, and over the mountains. I've never seen mountains. I imagine them implacable and bracing, I imagine them as giant rocky shoulders tensed in barricade. I imagine the trail behind me littered with debris, obstructed, obscure. I imagine Maiia at five swimming in the ocean, cutting the bottom of her foot on a barnacle. No place is without its dangers. I finger my money, all the edges soft from the anxiety of my restless fingers. The bored tinny voice in the loudspeaker announces the last boarding call for the bus to Thompson. The bus to Vancouver doesn't leave for another hour and a half. The city bus that would take me home stops on Portage up the street every twenty minutes. My heart pounds so loud I'm afraid it will wake Maiia up. My fingers feel electric. Something cracks open in my mind. Possibility stretches like a highway in front of me and all I have to do is find the courage to climb on.

Winnipeg Times-Dispatch

NEO-NAZIS CHARGED AFTER WITNESS COMES FORWARD

by Warren Mitchell, Police Reporter

Four years after Robert Michael Hawryluk was viciously beaten to death in a gay-bashing on the Assiniboine river walkway, four men have been charged in the killing. Police believe that all four men are members of a neo-Nazi organization called Wodin's Front. Although the men were suspects from the beginning, it has taken police four years to gather enough evidence to charge them with the crime.

"We have never seen anything like the disciplined wall of silence surrounding the skinheads," says Chief Investigator James Pollack. "After committing a serious crime people usually try to cover it up but that rarely works. In this instance, we believe there are many people, many skinheads, with knowledge of the murder, but no one talked for four years. These men almost got away with it."

The wall of silence cracked when an unidentified man, now living in Toronto, told some friends about the crime. The man identified other witnesses living in Winnipeg, and police were able to contact those witnesses, who then implicated the neo-Nazis.

Charged with first degree murder are Jason Adam Wilkes, 24, Michael Wallace Beston, 29, Thomas Marshall Friese,

24, and Jeffrey Dean Marks, 27, all of Winnipeg. Beston is believed to be a recruiter for the neo-Nazi organization. Marks and Wilkes both have prominent tattoos, including Thor's hammer on their necks, identifying them as members of Wodin's Front. Friese has a swastika tattoo on his ear, and all the men have spider web and other miscellaneous tattoos.

All four men are now in police custody. A trial date has not yet been set.

THIS CITY

I run into myself everywhere in this city. There I am waiting at a bus stop in the rain to go to Tom's mother's house when he moved there for a week. This city is remorseless in its inevitability. This city is full of apartments where I stand in front of the mirror blending concealer around my purple eyes. This city meets me everywhere at the door. This city street is where Carly and I sang on the sidewalk at the traffic, and everyone in this city heard us and kept driving. This city is full of slivers of me prone on the road and hiding in the train station. This city is relentless.

DEPARTURE

Bloated with snow and bulging with prefab housing complexes, swollen at the edges with townhouses, and punctuated by the nailed-up shack of the man who sells lost golf balls all summer, this misshapen city is tied up by the perimeter like a noose, like fishing line. This city is a snowy illusion pinned into position by the wet dreams of squabbling pigs in factory hog farms, by the incessant whispers of call centres, the lateral scaffolding of railway tracks, all the rusty graffiti-tagged cars marked with the caliphs of transience. The trains are pregnant with grain and other mysteries or else they are empty, another illusion. They do not speak the difference, there is no song, only clutter and clatter.

Without a car, this city is an island, a penitentiary circumscribed by orange city buses and their endless interlocking circuits, ponderous, full of disease. Downtown is the underwater grotto, abandoned pale-skinned people slipping silently in and out of the bank tower. The sidewalks are slippery with packed snow mottled with sand. I swim in and out of consciousness and I know everyone.

We are all the same person in the winter, one with an orange hat, one with red gloves. Our incestuous communal dreams rise and fall and writhe amid the thin grey exhaust of packing plants. This city is the destination of death for hogs and cows, the vortex that hungrily subsumes the debris of the prairie.

All these bridges arch hopefully over the rivers, long to be swallowed in the spring flooding, the silver kisses of fish and tree limbs, tires, and other river denizens. This city dreams of cracking ice and someone always drowns. The roads are decadent with potholes. Someone is always falling in or out and booster cables sleep in the trunk, someone is always driving away, dreaming of Kenora, Montreal, California.